*A*dventures on *A*melia *I*sland:

A Pirate, A Princess, and Buried Treasure

Also by Jane R. Wood

Voices in St. Augustine

Adventures on Amelia Island:

A Pirate, A Princess, and Buried Treasure

Jane R. Wood

Jane R. Wood

Florida Kids Press   ◆   Jacksonville, FL

Copyright © 2007 Jane R. Wood

Publisher's Cataloging-In-Publication Data
(Prepared by The Donohue Group, Inc.)

Wood, Jane R.
Adventures on Amelia Island : a pirate, a princess, and buried treasure / Jane R. Wood ; illustrations by Elizabeth A. Voils ; photographs by Ann Fontaine and Jane R. Wood.
– 2nd ed. – p. : ill. ; cm.
Includes bibliographical references.

ISBN-13: 978-0-9792304-0-0
ISBN-10: 0-9792304-0-3

1. Amelia Island (Fla.)--History--Juvenile fiction. 2. Princesses--Juvenile fiction. 3. Pirates--Juvenile fiction. 4. Treasure troves--Juvenile fiction. 5. Kingsley, Anna, 1793-1870--Juvenile fiction. 6. Amelia Island (Fla.)--History--Fiction. 7. Princesses--Fiction. 8. Pirates--Fiction. 9. Buried treasure--Fiction. 10. Historical fiction.

I. Voils, Elizabeth A. II. Fontaine, Ann. III. Title.
PS3573.O59 A38 2007
813.6

Library of Congress Control Number: 2007900206

Published through:

Florida Kids Press, 11802 Magnolia Falls Drive
Jacksonville, FL 32258
904-268-9572

To Terry

Acknowledgements

I owe thanks to many people and groups who provided assistance in writing this book.

The Research Library at the Amelia Island Museum of History; Dickie Anderson, docent at the Amelia Island Museum of History and local author; Kingsley Plantation park ranger, Roger Clark; Fort Clinch park ranger, George Berninger; members of the Fernandina Pirates Club, especially Lawrence Mackie (Larmacdawg), Paul Mathews (Mad Max), Christopher Hamick (Slappy) and Steven Hair (Capt. Steve); The Palace Saloon manager Hupp Huppman and the Sheffield Family; fellow author Pamela Bauer Mueller and her husband Michael; editor Carey Giudici; a very special 4th grade teacher, Linda Smigaj; my dear friend and photographer Ann Fontaine; and my colleague, good friend, and very talented graphic designer Beth Voils.

I owe special thanks to many members of my family who have assisted and encouraged me in so many ways. My sister Priscilla, my nephew John, my nieces Emily and Lindsey, my daughter-in-law Jennifer, my two sons Jonathan and Brian, and especially my husband Terry.

Chapter 1
Spring Break

"Singing Christmas songs in May is just plain dumb," Bobby said. He crossed his arms over his chest and stared defiantly out the window of the family minivan.

Five-year-old Katy ignored her older brother and sang even louder.

"Jingle bells, Jingle bells, Jingle all the way. Oh, what fun it is to ride in a one-horse open sleigh. Hey!" She shouted the word "hey" and threw a fist in the air.

Katy turned to look into the backseat.

"Mom, Bobby's not singing."

"Why would I want to sing a stupid Christmas carol at this time of the year?" Bobby said. "Besides, this is Florida. Who ever heard of a sleigh ride in Florida?"

"That doesn't matter. It's just a song. I like *Jingle Bells* because we know all the words," Katy said. "Would

1

you rather sing something else?"

"No, I'd rather be fishing. Singing is dumb," he said.

"It's not dumb and it makes the time go faster when you're riding in a car." She paused. "Besides, Mom said we're going to do things together this week. What do YOU want to do?"

Bobby thought about that for a moment. "I'd like to play first base for the Chicago Cubs, or fly to Alaska and pan for gold, or go deep sea fishing and catch a hammerhead shark or … "

"You wish!" his older brother Joey said sarcastically. Joey was thirteen and loved to tease his nine-year-old brother. "What would you do with a hammerhead shark if you caught one?"

"I'd call all the TV stations and newspapers and get 'em to do a story on me," he said. "I can see the headlines now. *Local boy catches record-breaking shark.* ESPN will interview me. I'll show everyone the scars I got when the shark attacked my arm as we were bringing it into the boat. I'll tell them it took me four hours and twenty-three minutes to reel it in. I'll pose for pictures and then sell my story to *Sports Illustrated*. They'll pay me thousands of dollars for an exclusive interview."

Joey laughed. "You've got a wild imagination. It makes me wonder if we can believe anything you say."

"At least my life will have some adventure in it. You're probably going to be a stupid accountant or banker or something boring."

"At least I'd be earning a living instead of running off like Indiana Jones."

As they started to cross the bridge going over the St. Johns River, they saw a large cruise ship off to their left leaving the cruise terminal.

"Look kids," their mother said. They were all silent as they watched the huge ship navigate its way toward the ocean. "Maybe one of these days we can take a cruise to the Caribbean. Now, wouldn't that be an adventure?" she said.

The three kids were lost in thoughts of travel on the high seas as they watched the ocean liner come in their direction. Katy was thinking about the people who were on board and imagining what it would be like to be there. Joey was amazed at the size of the ship and was wondering if it would clear the bridge. He was surprised to see how close it came to the bottom of the bridge. And Bobby was thinking about pirates.

"Mom, are there still pirates today—like we hear on the news?" Bobby asked.

"Yes, there have been some incidents, but those are mostly in other parts of the world and on smaller boats. I think it's pretty safe here, especially on a ship that size."

"What do pirates do?" Katy asked, wide-eyed.

"They steal your money and make you walk the plank. Or if they're in shark-infested waters, they throw people overboard," Bobby said dramatically, as he grabbed his throat and made drowning sounds. "Glug, glug, glug!"

"Bobby, don't say things like that. You'll scare your sister," their mother said.

"You don't have to worry about any pirates around here, Katy," Joey said. "I'll protect you. And if we do run into any, we'll let them have Bobby."

"Very funny," Bobby said. "Only, you'll be soooo jealous when I return many years later with tons of money. I'll become an expert on shipwrecks and search for buried treasure. I'll find gold doubloons and all kinds of jewels. I'll give Katy a real diamond tiara and buy Mom a new house. And you, my dear brother, I'll give you one shark's tooth."

"You're such a dreamer. You know you're never going to do any of that stuff."

Bobby didn't bother to reply. He was watching the ship as it sailed under the bridge. They were all watching as Katy started humming *Row, Row, Row Your Boat.*

Chapter 2
Kingsley Plantation

The van turned north on a meandering road that ran along the north bank of the river. They could still see the cruise ship off in the distance, but soon it was out of sight. Their attention shifted to new sights along the two-lane road.

They passed several fish camps selling bait, fresh shrimp, and soft drinks. Many of the homes along the river had piers that extended out into the water, and some had colorful mailboxes decorated as fish, or manatees, or pelicans. They crossed several bridges, and saw people fishing—some from the bridges, some from the shore, and some from boats.

"I love this drive," their mother said. "There's so much natural beauty here."

Long stretches of road were lined with sabal

palms, pine trees, and palmetto bushes. White egrets were looking for their next meal in the tall grasses of the marshes that flanked the roadway. Patches of wildflowers peeked out from the underbrush, adding splashes of color to the scenery.

As they approached the Mayport Ferry landing, their mother announced that they would stop at Kingsley Plantation so she could get some information for a story she was writing. Jennifer Johnson was a writer who wrote articles for magazines and newspapers. As a single mother, she often brought one or all of her kids with her when she was researching a story and always tried to make it a learning experience for them. Once when she was doing a story in St. Augustine, she helped Joey find a topic for a history project.

"I need to talk to one of the park rangers before it closes at 5:00," she said. "I've got to get some details on the plantation house which they say is the oldest one still standing in the state of Florida. You kids will see some real Florida history today."

She turned into the Timucuan Ecological and

Historic Preserve and followed the signs that led to Kingsley Plantation. They bumped along the narrow dusty road that snaked its way through a heavily wooded area of pines, palms, and massive oak trees dripping with Spanish moss.

Occasionally, they saw a creek or stream that led to the marshes, but mostly there were thick trees and vines and bushes. In some places, the limbs from the huge oak trees reached completely across the road, so that their van seemed to be going through a tunnel. Katy began counting the number of butterflies she saw, and Joey pointed out an armadillo that scooted across the road.

"This looks like a rainforest," Bobby said, and gave his version of a Tarzan yell while pounding his chest with his fists.

Jennifer looked at him in the rearview mirror and gave him the "that's enough" look.

"From what I've read, many of these trees were not here when the island was a plantation. They cleared much of the land so they could cultivate the crops," she said.

"What's a plantation?" Katy asked.

9

"I know what that is," Bobby said. "We just studied about them in school. It's like a big farm."

"That's right, Bobby," his mother said.

"So what did they grow here?" Joey asked.

"Indigo, sugar cane, corn, and a special kind of cotton called Sea Island cotton. The cotton was a valuable cash crop because of its strong fibers, but it took slaves many hours to pick it and remove the seeds before it was sent to market. When slavery was abolished, it was no longer practical to grow it. It became too expensive to harvest it."

"They had slaves here?" Bobby asked, his eyes widening.

"Yes, in fact, just ahead are the remains of some slave cabins that were built in the 1800s," she said. "We can stop and look at them on the way out, if you want."

The van grew quiet as they drove past the ruins.

Chapter 3
A Real Princess

Because it was late in the afternoon, the park was getting ready to close. Jennifer parked the van and told the boys to explore the grounds while she went to the ranger's office.

"I'll take your sister with me," she said. "You might want to check out the garden or the old barn. There are exhibits you can read that will give you information about this place. The house is closed for some preservation work, but you can walk down by the water. Just don't go into the water, please," she said, looking directly at Bobby.

"Got it," he replied and gave her a thumbs up.

Jennifer held Katy's hand as they walked along the path toward the old plantation house.

"Who used to live here?" Katy asked.

"Several families owned the plantation over the

years, but the most memorable one was the Kingsleys. Zephaniah Kingsley and his wife Anna lived here in the early 1800s. It's rumored that Anna Kingsley was once an African princess."

"A princess from Africa?" Katy said in amazement. "I didn't know they had castles in Africa."

Jennifer laughed. "She was not the kind of princess you read about in fairy tales. Historians think her father was a nobleman in Africa, but he lost a dispute when he tried to become king, and all his possessions

and family were taken from him. Anna was captured and sold into slavery at the age of thirteen."

"Then what happened to her?"

"She was sent to Cuba on a slave ship where she was bought by Zephaniah Kingsley. He was a planter and a slave trader. Obviously, he was very impressed with her, because he married her and gave her many responsibilities in the running of his plantations. It's a very interesting story, even better than many fairy tales because this one is true."

"Wow," Katy said, looking around and trying to picture it all. "And she lived right here?"

"Yep. For part of her life, anyway. When Florida became a United States territory, laws were passed that restricted the activities of black people. So Anna moved to the island of Haiti where Zephaniah had started a colony. After he died, Anna returned to Florida and lived near here until she died."

"Do you think she lived happily ever after?" Katy asked.

"I don't know about that, but she was a strong

woman who achieved some remarkable success at a time when most black women had little freedom or opportunity to improve their lot in life."

"Maybe you can do a report on her for school some day. There are some books about her in the book store. If you see one you like, I'll buy it for you and we can read it together."

"I like stories about princesses," Katy said.

Chapter 4
A Different Time

When Jennifer finished meeting with the park ranger, she and Katy walked toward the Fort George River where the boys were throwing rocks into the water.

"Did you boys learn anything new today?" Jennifer asked.

"Yeah, I learned my brother is a geek. He read every word on the exhibit in the barn," Bobby said.

"Did you know that some of the tabby walls of that old barn are two hundred years old?" Joey said. "And there was a lady here who started out as a slave but got her freedom and then owned some slaves of her own? That's weird."

"You have to remember it was a different time. People thought differently then. Planters needed slaves to be able to work their plantations. Slavery was a ter-

rible thing, but the plantation owners provided them with homes, food, and security, and sometimes even gave them their freedom."

"Let's stop at the slave quarters we passed on the way in. Some information boards there will give you some more details of what their lives were like."

They drove the short distance to where the remnants of the slave cabins were still standing. The twenty-three structures were arranged in a semi-circle—the same way villages were designed in West Africa. The homes were made out of tabby, a mixture of oyster shells, sand, and water. Each one had a fireplace where the families could prepare their meals.

"It says here the plantation owner allowed them to grow some of their own food on plots of land," Joey said, pointing to one of the exhibit boards. "But I still don't understand how people thought it was right to own other people. I'm glad times have changed."

"Me too," Katy said.

"Speaking of food," Bobby said. "I'm starving! When are we going to eat?"

"We're leaving in a few minutes," Jennifer said. "My friend Annie is expecting us about 6:30. And if I know Annie, she's going to have supper ready."

"I hope it's not yams, and okra, and black-eyed peas. I could go for a big juicy burger."

"Well, whatever it is, you'll eat it," his mother said in a serious tone. "Annie's invited us to stay for the whole week. I'm working on a story about the Isle of Eight Flags Shrimp Festival, which is next weekend. There will be a parade and an art show, and of course, lots of shrimp. I understand they even have a pirate invasion one night."

"Cool!" Bobby said.

But Katy was not saying much. She didn't like all the talk about pirates. She'd rather hear nice stories where the people all lived happily ever. Maybe she could find a pirate story with a happy ending. *That would be nice*, she thought.

Chapter 5
Katy and the Pirate

They got to Annie's house about an hour later. Annie and Jennifer were old friends. Annie was a professional photographer who had worked with Jennifer on many of her stories.

Annie and her husband lived alone in a large two-story house that looked out over a marsh. All of their kids were grown and gone. When Jennifer had called Annie to tell her she was doing a story on the annual Shrimp Festival and asked if she would take some photos for her, Annie had suggested that she bring the kids and stay for the week.

"It will be nice having kids around for a while," she said. "And you and I can spend more time together working on the story if you aren't driving back and forth."

Jennifer had asked the kids if they'd like to go, and

19

when she got two enthusiastic responses and one "maybe," she decided it might be good for all of them. Many of their friends were going away on exciting trips during their spring breaks, but she just couldn't afford any vacations right now. This would give them a change of scenery for the week and maybe an adventure or two.

The kids were originally supposed to spend the week with their dad who lived several hours away, but he had a business trip come up unexpectedly, so they had to postpone their visit. Their parents had divorced several years earlier.

They got to Annie's house before dark. Annie, who was older than Jennifer, greeted them from the front porch. She gave Jennifer a warm hug, and introduced herself to the kids. They mumbled polite hellos. Katy thought Annie smelled like cinnamon and reminded her of her grandmother.

"Make yourselves at home here,"Annie said."Just be careful in the backyard. We sometimes get critters from the woods. They mean no harm, but if they get scared, they will protect themselves."

"What kind of critters?" Katy asked.

"Oh, all kinds of things. We have a family of raccoons who like to check out our garbage cans on a regular basis. We see all kinds of birds from our back porch, and sometimes a deer or two will wander through." She didn't mention the snake she and her husband had killed the day before. "Just watch your step. Don't try to sneak up on something, and you should be OK."

Katy slid her hand into Joey's.

As predicted by Jennifer, Annie had a full meal prepared. To Bobby's delight, it was spaghetti, one of his favorites. Jennifer asked the kids to help her unload the car before it got dark.

Joey started handing out bags and backpacks.

"Who put you in charge?" Bobby complained.

"I'm the oldest, and everyone knows the oldest is the smartest," Joey said. "And because I'm bigger, I command respect."

"You're not in command of me," Bobby said with his hands on his hips.

Katy didn't like it when her brothers started

bickering. "Joey, give me something to carry. Bobby, the sooner we get everything in the house, the sooner we can eat," she said in a scolding tone.

Joey handed her a pillow and her stuffed teddy bear. She turned on her heel and went inside.

Annie was giving directions on the sleeping arrangements. "Jennifer, you and Katy can sleep upstairs. The boys can share the room off the living room. Make yourselves at home. I'm going to go check on the spaghetti."

Katy climbed up the stairs. There was a large open area at the top that looked like somebody's workspace. One wall was covered with photographs from all over the world; another had a big window looking out over the backyard. A large wooden table in the middle of the room was covered with papers and photographs. There was a computer and printer, several file cabinets, and bookshelves loaded with boxes and photo albums.

She walked through the room slowly, trying to take it all in. An open door led to a bedroom with pale blue walls, white ruffled curtains, and a canopy bed. Katy

22

had never slept in a canopy bed before. She giggled as she placed her teddy bear on one of the pillows.

Just then, her mother came in. "You like it, sweetie?"

"Mom, this is so pretty!" Katy said. "I've never slept in a bed like this before. I'll be just like a princess."

Jennifer smiled and gave her a quick squeeze. "I bet I won't have any trouble getting you to go to bed tonight," she said. "Why don't you wash up for dinner while I make one more trip to the van? Then we'll see if we can help Annie in the kitchen."

Katy went into the adjoining bathroom to wash her hands. While drying them, she peeked out the window. What she saw in the backyard of the house next door made her gasp.

A tall muscular pirate was standing in the middle of the yard. A buccaneer hat covered his long dark hair that flowed past his shoulders. He wore a black vest over a white shirt with long puffy sleeves that made his arms look huge. A thick black belt at his waist held an evil-looking dagger. He was waving a shiny sword back and forth and thrusting it forward as if he was stabbing something or someone. As he turned in her direction, she jumped back from the window.

Katy couldn't believe her eyes. But she was sure she had seen him. She had to make sure he was real. She gathered her courage and peeked out the window from behind the curtains. But the backyard was empty. There was no one there.

Had he been real? Or was her imagination playing tricks on her?

Chapter 6
Ants in His Pants

Annie's kitchen was buzzing with noise and activity. Jennifer was cutting tomatoes for the salad while Annie put a pot of water on the stove for the spaghetti. The boys, hovering over the cheese and crackers that Annie had put out on the counter, were being entertained by a large orange cat zigzagging between their legs and meowing loudly.

Katy quietly slipped into the kitchen and walked toward the window that faced the house next door. Her mother asked her to help set the table.

"The dishes are in the cupboard next to the refrigerator, and the silverware is in the drawer next to the sink," Annie said.

"Joey, help your sister with the dishes. She can't reach that high," Jennifer said. "Make sure you wash

25

your hands first."

Annie's husband, George, came into the room. He was a tall man with dark hair streaked with grey. He stood near the doorway and scratched his chin as he surveyed the activity. "What have we here?" he said. "We could open a bed and breakfast with all this help."

"Everyone, this is George," Annie said. "He lives here, but don't pay any attention to him. He tells stories, and you can't believe a word he says."

"Aw, that's not true. All of my stories are based on fact. I might exaggerate a little now and then, but that makes 'em more interesting," he said. "What can I do to help?"

"We'll need some extra chairs for the table. Why don't you and Bobby take care of that?" Annie said.

"Right-o," he said. "C'mon, Sport. I'll show you where we keep the special chairs." George led him down the hallway to a spare room with a large closet.

"What's so special about them?" Bobby said.

"Well, that depends. Some are for people that we like, and some are for people that we don't like.

Fortunately for all of you, we like you. Otherwise, you'd be in deep trouble."

"What kinda trouble?"

"Oh, can't rightly say. You see, the chairs decide what to do with the people we don't like. Why, once, there was a salesman here who wouldn't leave us alone. He was showing us all kinds of gizmos that we didn't need. I sat him at the kitchen table at one of these chairs, and before long, he started fidgeting something awful. He acted like he had ants in his pants. And you know what?" George said.

"What?"

"He did have ants in his pants. I don't know where they came from, because Annie does not allow bugs in her house, but he quickly made his excuses and left."

George shrugged his shoulders and chuckled as he pulled two folding chairs from the closet. "He was scratching and squirming all the way to his car. We never heard from him again."

Bobby looked at him curiously. "I think you're making it all up. I bet you put something in the chair to make him itch. Or maybe there wasn't even a salesman. I think your wife is right. We can't believe a word you say."

"That's fine with me," George said. "Believe what you want."

He handed one of the chairs to Bobby who examined it carefully before taking it. George took the other chair and turned to go back to the kitchen. When George left the room, Bobby checked inside the closet for bugs.

Chapter 7
Graveyards and Buried Treasure

After supper, they all sat on the screened porch eating brownie sundaes. Bobby had a dribble of chocolate sauce on his shirt; and Katy was mixing her sundae until it looked like chocolate soup. Joey had finished his and was petting the cat.

"Be careful not to drop any of your ice cream on the porch. It will attract ants," Jennifer said.

Bobby looked at George who winked.

"Annie, this is the best brownie sundae I ever ate. Can I have your recipe?" Bobby said.

Jennifer interjected, "It's *may* I have your recipe, not *can*."

"Whatever," Bobby said. "I want to add it to my list of Super Duper Recipes I plan to sell so I can make a million dollars, and then I can go on an expedition to hunt for hidden treasure."

Annie laughed and said she'd be glad to give him the recipe. "What's everybody going to do tomorrow?" she said.

"I need to go into town and schedule some interviews in the morning. Then if the weather is good later, we could go to the beach for a few hours,"Jennifer said.

"Sounds like a plan,"Annie said. "Feel free to leave the kids here in the morning, if you'd like. I'll be here till lunchtime. Then I've got to go shoot some pictures in an old cemetery, but George should be here all day." George nodded.

"You're going to take pictures in a graveyard?" Bobby asked in amazement.

"Yeah. There's a lot of history there that goes back to the 1700s. I've been asked to help document it in case a hurricane or something destroys some of the headstones."

"Isn't it spooky in there?"Katy said.

"Nah. I'm not scared,"Annie answered. "But I'll tell you what. If you want to hear some scary tales, then you should take the ghost tour in town that our history museum puts on. I've done it before, and it's a hoot."

"Are there really ghosts here?" Bobby asked.

"According to legend, there are," George answered. "That's all part of a city's history—legends, gossip and tales. There are lots of things you hear about that you can't prove, but it sure makes for some interesting stories."

Joey exchanged looks with his mother, remembering the voices he had heard in St. Augustine. He never did find out if there was a logical explanation for them— that they really belonged to someone in the near vicinity, or if they were voices from the past. It was still a mystery, and Joey thought about it often, especially when other things came up that couldn't be explained.

They all sat there listening to the night sounds. When the tree frogs and the crickets started their high-pitched chirping, it sounded like a well-rehearsed chorus. An owl hooted off in the distance, and the cat purred loudly, adding to the symphony of sounds.

"Annie, are there really pirates on Amelia Island?"

Katy asked.

"There used to be," Annie said. "Because of the nearby islands and the deepwater harbor, it made it a good hideaway for outlaws and pirates. There are lots of stories about pirates and buried treasure here."

"Buried treasure! For real?" Bobby said.

Everyone laughed. Jennifer shook her head. "I'm afraid you've opened up a can of worms now."

"Aw, c'mon. Tell me about the buried treasure," Bobby said.

George pulled his chair closer to Bobby's. "Tell you what. I've got some books and old news articles in there that tell about Fernandina's early days. I'll get them out tomorrow, and we can go through them. How does that sound?"

"Cool. Hey Mom, I'll do some historical research of my own."

"That's great. And you might actually learn something. But that will have to wait until tomorrow. It's time for bed. Go get into your pajamas and I'll come say good night in a minute."

"Mom, can I check my e-mail on your laptop before I go to bed?" Joey said.

"Joey's got a girlfriend," Bobby chanted. "Joey's got a girrrlllfriend."

Joey dismissed his brother with a dirty look. "Can I? I'm expecting an e-mail from Boston," he said.

"Sure, just don't take too long. And remember, it's *may* I," his mother said.

The boys left, slamming the porch door as they went back into the house. Katy crawled into her mother's lap.

"Can I go to bed when you do?"

The adults exchanged glances and grins.

"Sure. I'm pretty tired anyway, and I want to get started early tomorrow," she said. "Thanks, Annie and George. I can see already that this is going to be an interesting week. Cemeteries, pirates, and buried treasure, oh my!" She winked at them as she scooped up Katy and headed to bed.

"Good night and sweet dreams," Annie said.

George added, "Don't let the bedbugs bite."

Chapter 8
Buried Treasure

The next day Bobby was up earlier than usual. He dressed so quickly, his t-shirt was on inside out. He charged into the kitchen and found George reading the morning paper.

"I'm ready," Bobby said. "When do we start?"

"Whoa, Sport. I haven't had my second cup of coffee yet, and you haven't had anything to eat. You know what they say about breakfast—it's the most important meal of the day. Those news articles aren't going anywhere."

"Yeah, but what if someone else gets to the treasure before we do? Just think how mad you'll be."

"Yep," George said, as he turned the page and took another sip of coffee.

Bobby could see that he was going to have to be

patient, so he poured himself some Rice Krispies and sat in a chair at the other end of the table. Annie brought him a glass of orange juice and said his mother had already gone to the museum, but she would be back in a few hours.

Soon Katy appeared at the table with her teddy bear.

"How did you sleep last night?" Annie asked her.

"Like a princess," she said with a big smile. Her blue eyes sparkled with delight.

"Would you like some breakfast? How about some pancakes? I'm an expert pancake maker."

"I would love some. Can I help? I help my Grandma make cookies all the time."

As Annie let Katy stir the pancake batter, Joey came into the room and joined the others at the table. He asked George if he could see the sports page.

"Are you a Jaguars fan, Joey?" George said.

"Of course. But my favorite sport is baseball. I pull for the Red Sox."

"I'm a Cubs fan myself. You're lucky your team

has made it to the World Series in recent years. They even won! We Cubs fans have had a long dry spell."

"I know what you mean," Joey said.

"Speaking of being lucky," Bobby interjected. "Where do you suppose we could find some of those buried treasures?"

George chuckled. He set his paper down and looked off into the distance. "Well, let's see. If I remember correctly, there were some stories about people finding some gold coins near Fort Clinch." Then he scratched his head and added, "I've got a brochure on Fort Clinch around here somewhere."

"Where's Fort Clinch? Is it near here? What happened there? Can we go there?" Bobby fired his questions with a sense of urgency.

George didn't answer. He just kept talking. "And then there's a story about an iron chain tied to a tree. Some people claim that it was left there by pirates to mark the spot where they buried their treasure so they could find it again.

"You know, pirates didn't use banks. They'd hide

their money in remote places and plan to come back and get it some day. But the life of a pirate was dangerous. Many of them never made it back."

"So what kinda treasure did they hide?" Bobby asked.

Katy had finished her cooking duties and had crawled into Joey's lap. The three of them were entranced by the stories they were hearing. Annie, who was flipping pancakes, just grinned and shook her head.

"I'm sure there were gold coins, pieces of eight, gold ingots, jewels, anything of value that they could take. Ships were always sailing off the coast of Florida on their way to the Caribbean Islands. Others came here from Europe. There was a lot of trade going on, and trade always required some form of payment."

"What's an ingot?" Katy asked.

"An ingot is metal that's been cast into a mold. These would be gold bars."

"Whoa!" Bobby said. "You mean there could be gold bars out there somewhere on Amelia Island?"

"Could be," George said. "They even claim that

the famous pirate Blackbeard spent some time on Amelia Island and that his treasure is still here."

For a few moments the only sound that could be heard was the ticking of Annie's kitchen clock. Bobby's mouth was open. Katy was squeezing her teddy bear, and Joey looked at George in anticipation waiting for him to continue. George was enjoying every minute of it.

"Do you know why people were so afraid of Black-beard?" he asked.

"Because he was mean and scary?" Katy said.

"Basically, that's it. He was a big man with a thick, black beard. He wore a black hat and would sometimes light fuses under it, so smoke and a red glow would appear around his face. They say he would sometimes shoot one of his crew just to remind the rest who was boss."

Katy, who slid down further behind the table until she was halfway under the checkered tablecloth, was squeezing her teddy bear even tighter.

"What happened to him?" Bobby asked.

"He met his doom in a grisly way. He got shot in the face during a battle on a ship that he and his band of pirates had boarded. He continued to fight even after being shot until his head was nearly severed from his neck. After he died, the captain of the ship chopped off his head and hung it from the bow of the ship for all to see when they sailed back into the harbor."

"Ewwww," Katy said.

"Wicked!" Bobby said.

Joey just laughed. "Mr. Wells, I think your wife is right. You love to tell stories."

"You're right, Joey. But you can check the history books on that one. Just like your sister said. He was mean and scary."

"And rich," Bobby added. "And I'm gonna find his treasure!"

"Not until you finish your breakfast," Annie said. "But you can join me today if you want when I go over to the cemetery. You might have fun looking around there."

"Yeah. I'm going to go find that tree with a chain in it."

"Just be careful," George said. "They say those places are haunted by the pirates' ghosts protecting their property."

Bobby paused for a moment. "Aw, you're just trying to scare me. There's no such thing as ghosts."

And then he added quickly, "Joey, you want to go with me?"

Joey found the whole thing amusing. But he was also intrigued. He thought it might be kind of fun.

"Sure. I'll go with you. This could turn into a real adventure."

Chapter 9
Katy and the Pirate

Annie and the boys left for the cemetery after lunch. Katy was watching TV in the family room. George told her he would be in his workshop in the garage, working on a storage unit he was building for Annie's workroom.

"That woman has more projects than you can shake a stick at," he muttered. "You just call me if you need something, missy."

Katy watched an animal show on TV for a while, but then grew bored. She wandered out on the back porch to see if she could spot some real animals. She saw several birds hovering around a bird feeder hanging from one of the trees at the edge of the yard. She quietly opened the screen door so she wouldn't scare them off, and she sat down on the top step that was warm from the morning sun.

She noticed Annie's cat, Bootsie, crouching low in the grass, not far from the birds, and eyeing a cardinal busily pecking seeds from the grass. When the cat prepared to pounce on the unsuspecting bird, Katy jumped up from the porch waving her arms wildly and shouting, "Shoo, shoo, you naughty cat! Go away."

The bird flew away in a frenzy. Bootsie bolted in the other direction, darting under the hedges near the edge of the yard. Katy ran over to the shrubs, got down on her knees, and peered under the branches where the cat had disappeared.

"Oh, Bootsie. I'm sorry. Please don't run away. I was just trying to save the birds."

She crawled in the grass for several feet, but saw no sign of the cat. As she rose to her feet dusting off her knees, she did not notice the large figure looming on the other side of the hedge.

Suddenly, she saw him. There in a long black jacket, with beads braided into his hair, and layers of different colored chains hanging around his neck—stood the pirate.

Chapter 10
Bootsie's Friend

Katy screamed, her voice shrill with fear. But she could not move. Her legs were frozen in place.

The pirate threw one hand in the air as he cradled Bootsie in the other.

"Don't be afraid. I'm not going to hurt you," he said. "Is this your cat?"

Katy didn't know what to say. She just stared at him.

The pirate leaned over the bushes and dropped Bootsie gently on the ground next to Katy.

"There," he said. "Run along, matey. And leave my feathered friends alone."

Katy blinked. She finally found her tongue. "You like birds?" she said.

"I love birds, especially parrots. I had a parrot

once that spoke three languages."

Katy just stared at him. She folded her arms across her chest and tilted her head to one side.

"Are you for real?" she asked.

He threw his head back and laughed. "Yeah, I'm real. Wanna touch me?"

Katy jumped back. "No." Then she asked, "What are you doing here? Where did you come from? And why are you in the yard of a house where no one lives?"

The pirate pulled on his black beard. "Those are all good questions, little lady. I guess I'll answer them one at a time."

"First, I came from the marina. I have my boat docked there. Second, I've been thinking about fixing up this old place and living here. I used to come here as a kid. My uncle owned it, but he died several years ago and left it to me. I was never much interested, but I'm getting on in years and figured it was time to find a port to call home."

He looked around at the old house and then back at Katy.

"I like this town. The weather is good here, and the people are nice. And they have a keen appreciation for pirates. I like that."

"Are you gonna stay?"

"I think I might just do that. What do you think?"

"I don't know. I'm just a kid," she said as she waved at a mosquito buzzing around her head. "Aren't you hot in those clothes?"

He laughed again. "You sure ask a lot of questions. And yes, it is hot. Guess I'll have to find a more acceptable wardrobe," he said. "Do you live here?"

"No, we're just visiting my mother's friend for a few days. We live in …" but then she stopped herself.

"I'm sorry. I'm not supposed to talk to strangers."

"And that's a good policy. I won't ask you your name. I'll just think of you as Bootsie's friend," he said. "But you can call me Pete. Pete the Pirate. Nice to meet you, Bootsie's friend. I hope to see you again soon."

Katy didn't answer. "It was very, ah … interesting meeting you, Pete. I gotta go now. Mr. Wells will wonder what happened to me. Bye."

She turned and walked slowly back to the porch. When she got to the top of the steps she looked back, but he was gone.

Chapter 11
Graveyard Noises

Annie and the boys drove through the gates of the ancient cemetery. The sign in the front said Bosque Bello Cemetery, established in 1789. It was much larger than the boys had expected. There were headstones, and statues, and shrubs, and trees for as far as they could see. Annie drove to the back where the older graves were located. They parked under the shade of a large oak tree.

"You boys can look around, but don't wander off," she told them as she peered up through the trees.

"It should only take me about an hour to get what I need. It's starting to cloud up, and soon I'll lose the light," she said. "When I'm done, if we have time, I'll drive over to Fort Clinch. It's just down the road."

"Isn't that where they found some gold coins?" Bobby said.

"That's what they say."

"And what about the tree with the chain in it?"

"I don't know about that, but you can ask the park ranger. Maybe he'll know more about it."

Joey had already wandered off and was reading the gravestones. Bobby ran to catch up with him.

"Hey Joey, look at these graves. They have a fence around them. There's not much chance of anyone escaping from here," he said with a chuckle.

"You are a goofball," Joey said. "That's a family plot. All the people buried there are usually related."

He walked around to the front of the plot so he could read the marker. "Look at this one. This person was born in 1809 and died in 1880. He lived right through the Civil War. I bet he could tell some interesting stories."

They walked along the dusty road that curved through the graves and trees. Some of the headstones were so old it was hard to read the inscriptions, and many of the wrought iron fences were rusty with age. Some plots had angel statues, and many had broken wings or arms. The stumps of long-dead trees, probably struck by lightning or simply toppled over by old age, added to the graveyard's sense of history.

"Joey, what do you think happens to people when they die?"Bobby said.

"I guess the good ones go to heaven, and the bad ones go to you-know-where."

Bobby was unusually quiet for a while before he spoke. "Do you think there's such a thing as ghosts? You know, like what George was saying. That the ghosts of the pirates are protecting their treasures."

"Bobby, you're such a twit. First off, you're never going to find any buried treasure. And second, there's no such thing as ghosts. People just let their imaginations get the best of them. When weird things happen, they blame it on ghosts. There's usually a logical explanation for most things that happen."

Joey felt a little guilty about lecturing his brother about ghosts, when he himself had experienced something that he could not explain.

"Does everything have to be logical to you?"

"Yeah," Joey said. And then he added sheepishly,

"Most of the time, anyway."

"Well, not for me. I kinda like a little mystery. Makes life more exciting."

Just then a loud crash sounded behind them. Both boys jumped. A large branch had fallen from a tree about twenty feet away from where they were standing.

"Are you boys OK?"Annie hollered.

"Yeah, we're fine. It was just a limb from a tree," Joey answered.

"Well, be careful. This is a very old place. Everything is not as stable as it should be."

Bobby leaned over to Joey and whispered dramatically, "Hey, Joey, maybe that was one of these dead people trying to communicate with us. You know, like from one of these graves. Or maybe it was a warning from one of the pirates."

"Bobby, you're so full of it. That was just a coincidence. That branch just happened to drop while we were here."

"Yeah, well, maybe it was a coincidence, and maybe it wasn't. Just think about that, Mr. Logical," Bobby said. "Maybe someone is sending us a message."

"The only message I'm getting is that it's starting to rain. I'll race you to the car." They both started running, careful not to step on any graves.

Chapter 12
Fort Clinch

Annie paid the entrance fee into Fort Clinch at the ranger station and drove down the long road leading to the historic site. They passed bicycle paths and hiking trails, and signs giving directions to the campgrounds, the beach access, and the fishing pier. Before they reached the visitors' center parking lot and Annie could turn off the engine, Bobby was scrambling out the car door.

Annie and Joey followed, as Bobby raced down the path that led him to the fort. He barely noticed the drawbridge to the masonry fort, because he wanted to see what was inside. The fort opened into a large area surrounded by several brick buildings. What really got his attention were the large black cannons lined up along the outer walls.

Annie and Joey caught up with Bobby, standing in the middle of the courtyard.

"Joey, look at those cannons," he said with a big wave of his hand. "I bet they could sink a pirate ship."

"Is that all you can think about, pirates?" Joey scoffed. "If you'd read the brochure that George gave us, it says Fort Clinch served as a military post during three different wars. Confederate forces and then Union troops occupied it during the Civil War. That's way more significant than any pirate stories."

Bobby just gave his brother a dirty look. "Let's go

see what that guy has to say," he said and headed toward a man in an old military uniform who was talking to some tourists.

"Let me ask him some serious questions about the history of the fort before you ask a dumb one about pirates and buried treasure," Joey said.

Bobby didn't like being told what to do by his older brother, but it made sense to find out more about the fort's history. He'd even act interested if he had to. He might even ask a question about it, just to show Joey that he wasn't stupid.

The soldier was already explaining to Joey that the construction started on the fort in 1847, but was never fully completed. It was built there to protect the deep-water port of Fernandina.

"What's that building over there?" Bobby asked.

"That's the soldiers' storage house," the soldier said. "They used it to store food, uniforms and blankets, some tools, and all kinds of things that were needed for living here.

"Those buildings over there are barracks where

the soldiers were housed," he continued. "We also have a bakery, a blacksmith shop, a lumber shed, and even a laundry."

"Hey, it's just like a mini-city," Bobby said.

"That's right, son. They had to live here, and so they needed all the things that people would need wherever they live."

"What did they do for money?" Bobby asked.

"Well, it's interesting that you brought that up. I just happen to have some money here in my pocket."

He pulled out some paper money in a plastic bag and let the boys examine it. He also showed them some silver coins.

"That reminds me …" Bobby started to say. Joey rolled his eyes and walked away. "Have you ever found any coins buried here?"

The soldier laughed out loud. "Are you talking about buried treasure?"

"Yeah."

"I never found any treasure here, but there are lots of stories. When the school kids come here on their field trips, they all want to know about the chain in the tree."

"Yeah, me too! Has anyone seen it?" Bobby said.

"Nope. Not to my knowledge. But I did have a friend who was digging in her garden near Old Town once, and she found a can with a bunch of old coins in it. I mean really old coins, like from the 1790s. Some were from Spain."

"Oh, yeah. Did she get rich?"

"Nah, she sold them and I don't know how much she got for them, but she was pretty excited when she found them."

"Where's Old Town?" Bobby asked.

"It's just up that way," the soldier said pointing to the south. "That's where the town of Fernandina was originally located until they moved it to its present location."

"They moved the whole town?" Joey asked in surprise.

"Yep. When they built the railroad that connected this area to the rest of the state, it was located farther south on the island. It made good business sense to move the town. So they did."

"And what about the pirates?"

"By then, things were getting more civilized and the golden age of pirates was fading," he said scratching his head. "But you know, people still come here looking for pirates' gold. Some claim there's millions of dollars buried along the Florida coastline."

"If you go up there on the outer wall and look out over the river, you can see why pirates found this a good place to hide stuff. Lots of sand dunes, scrub brush, and thick woods. And it's a big island."

Yeah, too big, Bobby thought.

"Thanks, mister. I learned a lot today."

"Well, good. That's my job," he said as he turned to walk away. And then he said over his shoulder, "Good luck."

"For what?" Bobby said.

"Looking for buried treasure. I get the feeling you're one of those kids that just might try to find some."

Bobby smiled and said, "Thanks." He waved and walked over to where Annie was sitting on a bench.

"Annie, how far is it to Old Town?"

Chapter 13
Royal Jewels

As Annie drove home, it started raining again. She had to inch along to avoid the deep puddles and fallen branches.

"I sure hope it doesn't rain like this for the Shrimp Festival this weekend," she said. "Maybe Mother Nature is getting it out of her system now."

By the time they got to the house, the rain had diminished to a drizzle. Joey offered to help Annie carry her camera gear into the house, but Bobby raced to the front door and then hesitated, not sure whether to knock or go right in.

"Go on in, you don't have to knock," Annie said. "Just wipe your shoes on the doormat, so you don't track any mud on the floor."

Katy was playing in the living room with the cat.

Bootsie, wearing the teddy bear's jacket, did not look happy. As soon as the cat saw Annie, she bolted down the hall.

"Well it looks like you found a new playmate," Annie said.

"Not exactly. I don't think Bootsie likes playing dress-up," Katy said. She glanced out the window at the rain and sat down on the floor with a heavy sigh. "I guess we can't go to the beach now."

Annie walked over to her and said, "Maybe we can find a good indoor activity to do. Have you ever made any jewelry, Katy?"

"No, why?"

"Well, I do it all the time. And it just so happens that I need to be working on some for the arts and craft fair at our church. How would you like to help me?"

"Really? You make real jewelry, and I can help?"

"Yep. This will be a good rainy afternoon project for us."

Joey and Bobby were already arguing over the remote control for the TV when George came in.

"Would you boys like to check out some of those pirate stories this afternoon?" he said.

"Yeah. That would be super," Bobby said. "Where are they?"

"Hold your horses, son. First, I'm going to put on a pot of my famous chili. I love a good bowl of chili on a rainy day, and I always make the chili around here. Wanna help?"

"Sure," Bobby said. "Can you tell us more pirate legends while we cook?"

"I bet I can remember a few more. C'mon." They headed for the kitchen.

Annie and Katy went upstairs to the workroom. From one of her cabinets Annie pulled out several trays filled with beads of all sizes, shapes, and colors. Some were made of glass or plastic, some of clay or stone, and some of wood. Another tray contained small gold and silver beads. There was a plastic bowl with various fasteners, loops, wires, and threads. She set out a pair of pliers, some scissors, and a packet of large needles.

"There. Now we can begin," she said. "I'm going

to finish this necklace that I've been working on. You can watch how I do it, and then I'll show you how to make one for yourself."

Annie began stringing some brown flat stones and separated them with small gold beads. After every fourth stone, she would add a bright aqua stone.

"That's for a bit of color," she said. "I'll make some earrings to match and a bracelet. What do you think?"

"It's beautiful, Annie," Katy said. "The prettiest necklace I ever saw."

Annie laughed. "I might have to make you my sales manager." For fifteen minutes, she continued to work on the necklace and explained every step of the process as she went. Katy watched in total amazement. A couple of times, she asked Katy to hand her another bead. When Annie proclaimed it finished, she asked Katy if she'd like to try it on.

"Can I?" Katy asked with excitement.

Annie fastened the necklace around Katy's neck. It was too big for Katy, but she ran to the mirror in the bedroom to admire it anyway.

"I love it! Can I make one for me?" she said as she came running out of the bedroom.

"Sure. You can pick out some beads, and we'll make a necklace that will be fit for a princess. There are some catalogs and jewelry magazines over there in the bookshelf if you want to look at some designs."

"No, I don't need them. I know exactly what I want."

Katy was running her fingers through a container of pink crystal-like beads. She held one up to the light and watched it sparkle between her fingers.

"I want these," she said. "I want a simple necklace. Nothing long or dangling—nothing showy. A princess must have that elegant look."

Annie smiled as she gathered a handful of pink beads. "This will be perfect. These beads are plastic, so they won't hurt you if they ever break. And they do catch the light just right."

Annie spent the next hour showing Katy how to string the beads. Katy would stop occasionally to admire her work. Just as they were adding the fastener to both ends, Jennifer returned.

"What are you ladies up to?"she said, as she looked over Katy's shoulder. "Wow! Did you make that?"

"Yes, ma'am. It's my original Pretty Pink Princess Necklace. I'll wear it on special occasions." She held it up so her mother could admire it. "Can I get a purse to go with it?"

Jennifer looked at Annie and laughed. "What have you started here?"

"At least she didn't ask for a tiara," Annie answered.

"I already have one of those,"Katy said. "I got it at my friend's birthday party."

"Why don't you put on your Pretty Pink Princess Necklace, and let's go downstairs and show the boys your new creation," Annie said. "George is cooking tonight. Maybe they've made a creation of their own."

"Probably a mess," Katy said as the three of them headed down the stairs.

Chapter 14
Pirate Legends

George, Bobby, and Joey were sitting at the kitchen table. It was piled high with books and magazines.

"Here's a good one," Bobby said. "It says here that William Kidd, better known as Captain Kidd, operated out of Fernandina for at least four of his expeditions. It also says he had members of his crew bury some of his loot near here and then he killed them so they couldn't dig it up or tell anyone else about it."

"That wasn't very nice," Katy said as she crawled into a chair next to Joey. Annie was making some cornbread to go with the chili, and Jennifer was making iced tea. Both ladies were listening to the pirate conversation with amusement.

"Well, Katy," George said. "You'll be glad to know that not everything they say about pirates is bad. It says in this book that they rarely made people walk the plank, and they were really a very democratic group. The crew would elect a captain to command them when they were going into battle. The rest of the time, the captain worked as a regular crew member."

"I believe that," she said. "I met a pirate today and he was very nice."

Everyone stopped for a moment and looked at her. When she realized everyone was staring at her, she looked from face to face.

"What?" she asked.

"Where did you meet this pirate?" Bobby finally said.

"Next door. He helped me find Bootsie, and he told me his name was Pete. Pete the Pirate." She said it all very matter-of-factly.

"But Katy dear, there's no one living next door. That house is vacant," Annie said.

"I know. He was just checking it out. He might want to fix it up and move in. He's tired of living on the water." She grabbed one of the books and started turning the pages before she continued.

"Oh, don't worry, Mom. I didn't give him my name. I told him I couldn't because he was a stranger and I was not supposed to talk to strangers. So he just called me Bootsie's friend."

She flipped another page in the book. "Are we going to eat soon? I'm getting hungry."

Jennifer looked at Annie. Annie looked at George. Joey and Bobby exchanged glances and smiled.

George finally broke the silence, "That sounds like an excellent idea, my lady. All hands on deck, mates. Let's get this table cleared off, or someone's going to find himself at the bottom of Davy Jones' Locker."

Bobby jumped up and saluted, "Aye, aye, Captain." Joey started clearing dishes.

George leaned over and whispered in Katy's ear, "Ahoy miss, take care to protect those fine jewels you're wearing. There's scoundrels about. You wouldn't want them to end up in a pirate's chest."

Katy giggled as she fingered her Pretty Pink Princess necklace.

"I wanna get a pirate hat and a sword this weekend," Bobby announced.

"There'll be lots of those things to buy at the Shrimp Festival," George assured him. "A lot of the kids dress up like pirates for the parade on Thursday. Maybe we can pick up a few things tomorrow. How 'bout I take the kids downtown so you ladies can work? I'll take 'em by the museum and we can go down to the marina."

"Isn't that where people keep their boats?" Katy asked.

"Sure is. There will be all kinds of boats there for this weekend."

"Great. Maybe I'll see Pete there," she said.

"That would be nice. I'd like to meet him," George said with a wink to the others.

And with that, they all sat down for chili and corn-bread.

"Can I have an extra ration of rum with my dinner?" Bobby asked.

"No rum for you, my little landlubber," Annie said. "But I think we can find a mug for your milk."

She poured some milk into a silver tankard for Bobby, who sloshed it back and forth before taking a big swig. When he finished, he had a large white moustache across his upper lip. He wiped his mouth with the sleeve of his shirt and gave a loud belch.

"Bobby! What do you say?" his mother scolded.

"I say, shiver me timbers. That was the best milk I ever drank."

Everyone laughed ... even his mother.

74

Chapter 15
Never on Wednesdays

The next morning the sky was clear and sunny. After breakfast, George and the kids headed downtown for what George called his Deluxe Tour of the City.

"Ladies and gentlemen, please fasten your seat belts. You are in for Mr. Wells's Wild Ride. First, we'll go by the Amelia Island Museum of History. Then, we'll stop at the marina and see if there's anything fishy going on there." He waited for the groans. "Get it, fishy at the marina?"

"We get it. It's just a little early for bad jokes," Joey said.

"I liked it, Mr. Wells," Katy said. "I think you're funny."

"Why thank you, Katy. I think you're funny too," he said. They both laughed.

George drove down Centre Street. "Ladies and gentlemen, this is the main street of the charming little Victorian village of Fernandina Beach. Some of the buildings date back to the late 1800s." He told them that many of the Victorian houses have been converted to bed and breakfasts. Many are still used as private homes today. He pointed out that the colorful structures are known for their decorative trims and large porches.

"We like our porches," he said proudly. "And I've been told that the more porches a house had, the more well-to-do the family was.

"There's the old courthouse, and over there is the post office," he said pointing to two buildings across the street from each other. "Both of those were featured in the movie *The New Adventures of Pippi Longstocking*."

"I love that movie," Katy exclaimed. "I didn't know they filmed it here."

"Yes indeedy. I'll take you out to Old Town later and you can see her house."

"Did you say Old Town?" Bobby said.

"Yep. That's where the original town of Fernandina was."

"Yeah, I know. The soldier at Fort Clinch told us about it yesterday. He wasn't a real soldier, but he acted like he was one. He told us all about how the town got moved."

"Sounds like you learned something yesterday," George said.

"Now you sound like my brother. Does everyone think I'm a twit?"

"Nope. I think you're kinda neat, Bobby," Katy said. "Except when you tickle me," she added.

They drove to the end of the street and turned left past the waterfront and marina.

"We'll come back here, but first I want you to see our Museum of History. It's actually a historic building that used to be the county's jail. They converted it to a museum many years ago. Not every town has a museum in its jail."

Several blocks later, they came to an old two-story brick structure. There were still bars on some of the windows. George parked the car and they went inside to see

some of the exhibits. They saw old photographs that gave them a peek into what the people and places looked like years ago. There was a mural and exhibit of a Timucuan Indian village, and another display showing artifacts from the Spanish missions that once existed on Amelia Island.

Katy liked the costumes and old dresses she saw in one room. George told her that Amelia Island was named after a princess—Princess Amelia, George II's youngest daughter.

"I like this place better every day," she declared.

Joey read about how Fernandina Beach is considered the birthplace of the modern shrimping industry. "Now I see why they have a shrimp festival here," he said.

Bobby wanted to know what was on the second floor.

"That's the research library," George told him. "If you want to do some serious historical research, that's where you'll go."

"All I want to find is some gold bars. Would they have any treasure maps up there?"

"I don't think so. But I do know how to get to Old Town. We could start your hunt for buried treasure there. Let's go find your brother and sister."

They left the museum and drove back to the marina. Preparations for the Shrimp Festival were already in full swing along the waterfront. A stage was being erected in a parking lot. Orange cones were standing at attention, ready to block off designated streets from car traffic. Workers with clipboards were bustling around, checking diagrams and lists, making sure everything was being placed in its proper location.

"I need to stop here for a minute," George said. "I've got a friend who will be working in one of the food booths this weekend, and I need to see if he needs help setting up. I won't be long, if you want to go down by the boats and see if they're catching anything today."

The kids walked to the end of the marina where the charter fishing boats and shrimp boats were docked. As the boys watched a group of fisherman admire their catch, Katy wandered over to one of the boats that was docked near there. It had *Pete's Dragon* painted on the side in bright blue letters.

There was a tall man in a Hawaiian print shirt, shorts, and flip-flops hosing down the deck of the boat. Katy stared at his back since she couldn't see his face. His hair was tied back in a ponytail, but there was no mistaking that black beard. As he turned to move an ice chest, he saw her.

"Why, if it isn't Bootsie's friend," he said when he saw her. "What brings you here? Are you all alone?"

"No, I'm with my brothers," she said. "Is this your boat?"

"Yes, ma'am. This is my home away from home. In fact, this IS my home. What do you think of it?"

"It's very nice, but isn't it kinda small?"

"Oh, that's right. You're the little lady who likes to ask lots of questions," he said.

He looked around the harbor and out to sea before answering.

"No, you see, that's my living room out there," he said pointing to the open water. "I can watch the sun rise and set. I can watch dolphins play in the wake of my boat, and I can go swimming and fishing whenever I want. I don't know of many houses that can offer that."

Katy thought about that for a while. "But don't you get lonely?"

"Never. You see, I'm always meeting new people when I come to places like this. And I have lots of old friends, too. If I want to go see them, I just pull up anchor and sail away."

"But what about being a pirate? Are you really a pirate or are you teasing me?"

"Oh, I'm a pirate all right, but just not on Wednesdays. Wednesdays are my day off. Even pirates have to have a day off. It can be very hard work you know, acting mean and scary. We have a reputation to uphold."

Katy smiled. "I don't think you're mean. Maybe just a little scary." She studied his face for a minute, and then looked at his boat, seeing it through new eyes.

"I gotta go. My brothers will be looking for me." And then as she started to walk away, she said, "My name is Katy. Will I see you at the Shrimp Festival this weekend, Pete?"

"I hope so, Katy. I'll look for you and try not to be too scary."

"Bye, Pete. See you later." She skipped down the dock back to where her brothers were looking at a large ugly grouper that someone had caught on a fishing boat.

Chapter 16
Just Like in the Movies

"You kids getting hungry? It's just about lunchtime," George said.

"I'm starving," Bobby said.

"You're always hungry, Bobby," Joey said.

"Hey, back off. I'm a growing boy. Besides, I need my strength to carry all the loot I'm going to uncover," he said as he flexed his arm muscles.

"Mr. Wells, I'm kinda thirsty," Katy said.

"Sounds like we need to rustle up some grub and liquid refreshment. What does everyone feel like eating? There's seafood, of course, but we'll get a bellyful of that this weekend. How about a pizza or some hamburgers?"

"I could go for a burger," Bobby said. "And fries. You can't eat a hamburger without fries. It's a state law, you know."

"Well, we don't want to break the law now, do we? Do hamburgers work for everyone else?"

Katy and Joey both agreed, so off they went to a local fast food restaurant. True to his word, Bobby ordered a hamburger, fries, and a Coke. Joey got a fish sandwich with a chocolate milkshake, and Katy wanted chicken nuggets with pink lemonade.

As they ate their food, George told them more about Old Town.

"We know there was an Indian village there in the 1600s. The Timucuan Indians date back some 2,000 years and lived in this area before the French, Spanish, and others came. They were tall, many over six feet, which was very tall back then. They tied their hair on the top of their heads in buns and ponytails, which made them look even bigger. Their fingernails and toenails were sharpened into points, and many had tattoos on their bodies, even on their lips. They cut themselves with shells to make the tattoos."

"Ewww," Katy said. "They sound scary."

"Sounds cool to me," Bobby said. "What happened

to them?"

"They all died out in less than a hundred years, many from sickness brought by the Europeans. Indians had no immunities against the white man's diseases, like measles and mumps. And their culture disappeared when they adopted the new way of life brought by the Spanish and the French.

Everyone was silent. Then Bobby said, "Tell us about Old Town."

"A fort was built on that site and was occupied by many different people, including the Spanish, the British, a soldier of fortune from Scotland, and even a pirate named Luis Aury.

"One of the really colorful things about Amelia Island's history is that it was a major center for smuggling in the 1800s. You see, all the ports in the United States were forbidden from importing goods from Europe as a protest against the British. But at that time, Florida was not yet a state. So all kinds of goods from Europe, and even slaves from Africa, were brought into Fernandina, and then smuggled into the states north of here through Georgia."

"So who was in charge?" Joey asked. "Wasn't any-one trying to stop it?"

"Like a lot of places in America during that period, it was governed by whatever group or country could take control of it. Amelia Island is called the Isle of Eight Flags, because it was occupied or governed by eight different groups in its early history."

"I guess that's why there were so many pirates here," Bobby said.

"You're absolutely right. Pirates would bring in goods to smuggle into Georgia, and often those goods had been taken from other ships. They made good profits, so a lot of money passed through here."

"And I'm going to find some of it," Bobby said confidently.

"Well, if that's the case, then we'd better get going," George said.

They finished their lunch and drove to Old Town at the northern end of the island. George had told them there wasn't much to see, but Bobby was still disappointed when all he saw was a wide-open field along the river.

"I thought you said there was a fort here," Bobby said.

"There used to be a fort here, but it's been gone a long time. Erosion has taken most of it away," George said. "But you can see how close it was to the river. You can actually see Georgia over there," he said pointing across the river.

"So I wonder where that lady found those coins that the soldier at Fort Clinch was telling us about."

"It was probably at one of those houses over there," George said, pointing to some homes nearby. "People still live here, and I've heard they find things from time to time."

Bobby walked around kicking the dirt, hoping to turn up something. Then he walked down by the river.

"I bet I know what he's looking for," Joey said.

"The chain," Katy said.

"Well, that's OK. It will keep him busy for awhile," George said, and he called out to Bobby not to go too close to the water.

"Katy, I've got a surprise for you. Turn around and look at that big white house." George pointed to a Victorian house across the street from the site of the fort.

Katy tilted her head and stared at the white two-story house. It had a red roof and green trim around the windows. A three-story tower extended up from the front door in the center of the house. A neat white picket fence lined the front of the property.

"That's it! There it is!" she squealed. "That's the Pippi Longstocking house. I hardly noticed it after seeing all those Victorian houses in town today."

"Yep. At least, that's the house they used in the movie. It was kind of exciting around here when they shot that movie. I remember the ice cream scene down on Centre Street. What a mess! It looked like there was ice cream everywhere," George laughed.

"Does anybody live in the house now?" she asked.

"Yes. Someone bought it a while back. We need to respect their privacy though."

"Oh yes, I know. I just want to sit here and look at it." She sat down on the ground cross-legged, put her elbow on her knee and her chin on her knuckles, and just stared.

"Mr. Wells, do you think we could rent the movie tonight? I'd love to see it again," Katy said.

"Actually, I think Miss Annie has a copy. We show it to the grandkids when they visit. I bet we could talk her into it. Maybe some popcorn too."

Chapter 17
Digging for Treasure

Bobby was exploring the shoreline, looking especially close at all the trees. He knew they all thought he was crazy, but he didn't care. He felt there must still be some undiscovered treasures to be found.

He walked as far as he could go without having to wade into the water—that would not be a good idea—then he turned and started walking down a dirt road. He passed several small houses before he came to one that caught his interest. The old wooden house had a large front porch and a big yard with a short fence around it.

An old man smoking a pipe was sitting in a rocking chair on the porch. The smoke curled up around his head, reminding Bobby of the descriptions he had heard of Blackbeard the pirate. He knew he wasn't supposed to talk to strangers, but this old guy looked pretty harmless.

"Hey, mister. Have you lived here very long?" he said.

The man pulled the pipe out of his mouth and said, "Who wants to know?"

"Me. I'm Bobby Johnson. I'm visiting here and … and I'm trying to learn more about the history of Amelia Island."

He was rather pleased with himself for coming up with that kind of an answer. He figured that might impress the old man.

The man took another puff on his pipe. He stood up and stretched, and then started down the front steps. He paused when he got into the bright sunlight, took a handkerchief from his back pocket, and wiped his forehead.

"Kinda humid today," he said as he looked at the sky. "Might rain again. We sure had a gully washer yesterday." He walked toward Bobby, limping slightly. He moved the garden hose out of the way with his foot.

"Now what was it you wanted to know?"

"I've heard some interesting stories about pirates

and stuff," Bobby said. He figured he better get right to the most important question, as he wasn't sure how long this old geezer was going to last. *He could kick the bucket any minute now*, he thought.

The man grinned and shook his head. "I bet you're looking for the treasure. We get people here all the time asking questions about pirates and treasures and gold doubloons." The man took a few more steps and sat down on a tree stump not far from the porch.

"I was just telling my daughter the other day that we should charge admission for people to dig in our yard. Why, once when I was putting in a vegetable garden—oh, about five years ago—I dug up some old coins … " he said, looking toward the back yard.

"That was the best garden. We got a bumper crop of tomatoes, okra, and squash. Do you like squash, young man? My daughter fixes the best squash casserole. I don't know what she puts in it, but I could eat a whole plateful." He stared off toward the river.

Bobby looked at him closely. The old guy was kind of friendly. Probably lonely. There didn't seem to be anyone else around. Just a big grey dog that was sleeping on the porch. The dog was so old, it didn't even bark when Bobby came up. *He's probably just as ancient as the old man,* Bobby thought.

Bobby decided it would be nice to talk with the guy a while. He figured he wasn't going to find any treasure here. Might as well be friendly.

"I like string beans. Yep, they're my favorite. And corn on the cob with lots of butter," Bobby said.

"Yeah, I know what you mean. I'm not supposed to eat a lot of butter. Doctor says it clogs my arteries. But I do like a little ham fat in my string beans. Gives 'em a little kick."

"Yeah. My mom sometimes puts bacon in ours. I like it when the bacon's real crispy."

They were both quiet for a minute. The dog got up and stretched, yawned, and sat back down.

"Would you like to see my garden?" the old man said. "Actually, it's not a garden yet. My leg's been bothering me, so I haven't been able to till the soil. But I hope to get around to it in the next week. It kind of keeps me out of trouble. You know what I mean?" he said with a wink.

"Oh yeah, I know about trouble. It kind of follows me around," Bobby said.

"C'mon. I'll show you where it is."

The man got up from the stump and walked around to the side of the house. Bobby opened the gate and followed the old man. He could see some wooden tomato stakes leaning against the side of the house, a dirt area that had once been a garden, and some remnants of a small fence.

"Guess I'll have to do something about that fence before I plant. It used to keep the rabbits and other critters out."

Bobby decided he might as well ask the guy what he really wanted to know. "You said you found some coins once."

The man grinned. "Yep." He didn't offer any more information.

"Over there where I put the tomatoes, and this year I'd like to try some melons. Watermelon is my favorite, but I've never had much luck with 'em. Now, back where I grew up in Georgia …" his voice trailed off. "Shucks, you don't want to hear all that."

"Mister, would you like me to fix that part of the fence for you? I think it just needs to be stuck back in the ground."

"Well, that would be right friendly. Yes sir, that would be nice."

Bobby found a stick to help scoop out some of the dirt for the post holes. He picked up the fallen pieces of fence and started matching them to their original places.

He didn't notice that the old man had gone back into the house. Bobby worked on one section and then moved on to another. He was actually enjoying the work. He kept thinking that he might be digging in the same place where pirates had once dug.

The old man returned with the dog walking lazily beside him.

As Bobby worked on the third section, he decided to dig the holes a little deeper so the poles would not come out so easily. He got down on his knees and started scooping the dirt out with his hands. When he turned his head to grab one of the fence posts, the old man tossed something into the hole and walked away.

Bobby matched up the fence parts, just as he had done before. When he went to place the first pole in the ground, he saw something at the bottom of the hole. He wiped the sweat from his brow with his arm and squinted down in the hole to get a better look.

At first he thought it was a rock. But it was too shiny for a rock. He reached in and grabbed the object. When he opened up his hand, he could hardly believe his eyes.

"Oh my gosh! Look at this," he said running over to the old man who was standing at the edge of the garden. "Look what I found! I think it's an old coin."

"Let me see that," the old man said. He turned it over several times and fingered it. "Yep, I've seen one of these before. Found one right over there by the clothesline. We dug up half the back yard, looking for more. But we only found a handful."

"Do you think it's real?"

"Oh, it's real all right. We took ours to a coin specialist. He said it was from Spain, probably around the late 1700s."

"Gosh, a real treasure! Can I take it to show to my mom and my brother and sister? I'll bring it back. I promise! I just want them to see it."

"Son, it would give me great pleasure if you'd keep it. I remember when I was your age and … well, never mind. I know what it's like to find something like this. You take it and enjoy it."

"Are you sure? It could be valuable."

"Yeah, I'm sure. You keep it. And you can tell your friends whatever story you want to. The bigger, the better. You make it a whopper of a story," he said with a chuckle.

"Thanks, mister," Bobby said as he looked at the old man with new respect. "I don't even know your name."

"They call me Old Henry. But Henry will do just fine."

"Well, thanks Henry. This has made this the best spring vacation I ever had. I'm glad I met you, Henry."

"Me too, son. Me too!"

Chapter 18
A Day of Discovery

Bobby went running back to the others, waving his arms and hollering, "Hey guys. Guys! You won't believe this."

As he got closer, Joey said, "Here comes trouble."

"Look! I found some buried treasure," Bobby shouted.

"Yeah, right," Joey said. "And I'm Santa Claus."

"No kidding. Look at this." He held up the coin between his thumb and forefinger. "It's a real Spanish coin from the 1700s, and I dug it up in this man's yard right over there," he said, pointing down the street.

"You were digging in a man's yard?" Katy said.

"Yeah, but I was helping him with his garden," Bobby said. "It's kind of a long story."

"We'd love to hear all about it. Why don't you tell

us the whole story in the car? We need to be heading back to the house. The ladies will wonder what's happened to us," George said. And then he added, "Bobby, may I look at that?"

Bobby gave the coin to George, who turned it over several times and tried bending it.

"Looks pretty authentic to me. I know a guy who can appraise it for you and tell you what it's worth."

"Wow. I can't believe it. I actually found some buried treasure."

Joey asked if he could see it too. He examined it, and then gave it back to Bobby with a high-five. "Way to go, dude," he said.

When they got back, Bobby bolted out of the car and ran into the house, forgetting to close the door behind him. He ran from room to room looking for his mother. When he heard laughter coming from the back porch, he charged toward the back of the house nearly tripping over the cat.

"Mom, look what I found!"

Jennifer looked over her shoulder as he burst

through the back door. She and Annie were sitting in two wicker chairs, rocking back and forth and drinking iced tea.

"Calm down and slow down. What have you got?"

"I found this coin in a man's backyard at Old Town. He said it's a Spanish coin from the 1700s and he said I could have it. Look!" he said, as he thrust it at her.

Jennifer and Annie looked at the coin and then at each other, and then they laughed.

"It looks like you found your buried treasure after all," Annie said. "I'm sure there's a story to go with this and we want to hear all about it."

Bobby was beaming as he told the ladies about how he met Old Henry, and how he helped him with his fence in his garden, and how he found the coin at the bottom of one of the holes. He talked so fast that his mother had to ask him to slow down several times. When he was finished, they examined the coin again and gave it back to him.

"George said he knows a man who can praise it

for me," he said.

"You mean appraise. That means to determine its value," Jennifer said.

"Whatever."

Joey and Katy joined them on the back porch. Joey gave his mother a smile and rolled his eyes. Katy announced that she had some exciting news too, although hers was not as good as Bobby's. She told her mother and Annie about seeing the Pippi Longstocking house. She described it in detail and then asked Annie if they could watch the movie that night. Annie said she'd have to find it but thought she had a copy floating around somewhere.

Just then George entered the porch. "I'll have to run to the store, Annie, and get some ice cream. You just can't watch that movie without eating ice cream. It's a state law, you know," he said, and elbowed Bobby in the ribs.

Chapter 19
Ghosts and a Gun-Toting Woman

The next morning everyone slept in. The kids had stayed up late to watch the movie. The adults joined them for a family evening, complete with ice cream and popcorn. After the kids went to bed, Jennifer worked on her story. Annie and George rummaged through the attic, looking for some pirate clothes that their kids had worn when they were young. Annie found a pink purse that had been her daughter's favorite. She set it aside for Katy.

The kids spent a lazy morning, just hanging out, as Joey liked to call it. He spent some time on the computer sending e-mails to Boston and checking the baseball scores. Katy squealed with delight when Annie presented the pink purse to her.

"This will go perfectly with my new necklace.

Thank you, Annie. You're like my fairy godmother," she said. Annie blushed and gave her a hug.

After lunch they all piled into Jennifer's van and drove into town which was already buzzing with excitement. The parade was scheduled to begin at 6:00, but the sidewalks were already filling up. They visited several stores so the kids could get at least one new item for their pirate costumes. Bobby was determined to find the perfect sword and hat.

Katy looked for gold necklaces. "I want several of them, just like Pete wears."

Joey whispered to his mother that he thought Katy's fantasy about seeing a pirate was getting out of hand.

"Don't worry, dear. She just has an active imagination."

"Yeah, she's been listening to Bobby too much. He's a bad influence on her."

Joey said he was too old to dress up like a pirate, but he did buy a red bandana which he intended to tie on his head. "I can be a biker. That's a little more mature than a pirate, don't you think?"

His mother just laughed. "You can be anything you want. It's your vacation."

By the time they finished shopping, lots of people had already set up chairs along the parade route. Annie said they should go find a spot and do the same thing.

"After we position our chairs, I'll take everyone on my special Deluxe Ghost Tour," George said.

"That might not be such a good idea for everyone," Annie said, pointing discreetly to Katy. "I've got special plans for Katy. You take the boys. I've got something I want her to see."

"I'll sit right here and save our spot," Jennifer said. "You go have fun."

Annie held Katy's hand as they crossed Centre Street and walked down Seventh Street. They stopped in front of a beautiful Victorian house with lots of windows and a big porch that wrapped around the front and side of the house. The veranda had several white wicker chairs and a porch swing big enough for two.

"I wanted you to see this house. Many years ago,

a lady named Kate Bailey lived there. Her husband built this house for her in 1895, when she was a new bride."

Annie explained to Katy that in those days, it was customary for a groom to build his bride a house. Kate had grown up near there just down the street. Her parents had given the couple the lot as a wedding present.

Annie continued her story. "Kate was a feisty lady. See that tree over there?" she said pointing to a huge oak tree on Ash Street.

Katie looked around. "You mean that one in the middle of the road?"

"Yep. They call that Kate's Tree," Annie said. "It's called that because she saved it. When the city wanted to pave the road, they said they'd have to cut down the tree. But Kate wouldn't let them do it."

"How did she stop them?"

"She got her husband's shotgun, sat on the porch, and threatened to shoot anyone who tried to cut it down."

Katy was wide-eyed. "Did she shoot anyone?"

"Nope. She didn't have to. And look, the tree's

still there. It just goes to show you that one person can make a difference," Annie said. Then she added with a giggle, "Course, she had a little help from her shotgun."

They walked over to the tree to get a closer look.

"Just think, Annie. Having a tree named after you. That's much better than a building or a football field. And George told me that this whole island was named after a princess. That's so cool."

A few blocks away, George was giving Joey and Bobby his special ghost tour.

"This is called the Silk Stocking District because the people who lived here were wealthy enough to afford silk stockings," George said. "But what's really interesting about this neighborhood is the number of ghosts that reside here."

Joey and Bobby exchanged nervous looks.

They walked for several blocks past many Victorian houses. George told stories about doors being opened and closed, dishes moving themselves, pictures coming down from walls, and dogs barking in the middle of the night for no apparent reason.

"They say dogs will live in a house with a ghost, but a cat won't," George said.

"That's just plain weird," Joey said.

"I agree, but there're plenty of residents here that have stories to tell about strange reactions from their pets." Then he added, "And it's not just the houses that are haunted. Some say the Palace Saloon is haunted by an old bartender called Uncle Charlie."

Bobby was silent for once, as they walked a few more blocks. Joey was also quiet, trying to make sense of it all.

Finally Bobby asked George, "Do you think there are really such things as ghosts?"

"I don't know, Bobby. But it's kind of fun to talk about, don't you think?" he said. "If we didn't have stories about ghosts and pirates and Big Foot and UFOs, life would be rather dull."

Then he added, "I can't prove that these things exist; but then again, I can't prove that they don't. I will tell you this—the general consensus is that the ghosts here are fairly happy ones. It seems they just don't want to leave, or they may have some unfinished business to tend to."

"Oh, that's good," Bobby said. "That will make Katy happy. She wouldn't like knowing there are unhappy ghosts here," he said sarcastically.

On that note, they started walking back to the center of town. They could hear the bands warming up, and a police siren off in the distance.

"Sounds like the parade is about to begin. We'd better get back and rescue your mom. An unprotected woman could be easy prey for scoundrels and scalawags. It's up to us to protect the womenfolk. Are you with me, me hearties?"

"Aye, aye, Captain. We're right behind you," Bobby said. "Arrr!"

Chapter 20
The Parade

The main street of Fernandina Beach had turned into a big party. People were calling across the street to their friends, laughing, and generally having a good time. Some had positioned themselves in chairs or were sitting on the curb of the sidewalk. Others filled the back of pick-up trucks parked along the parade route, giving them front row seats. Teenagers were weaving in and out of the crowds, looking for friends and collecting the colorful bead necklaces, just like at Mardi Gras.

Many younger kids were already dressed in pirate garb. Bobby and Katy quickly changed into theirs. Bobby slid his shiny new sword into his belt and placed his black felt hat firmly on his head. He wore a black vest and a shirt with long white sleeves that George had found in the attic. Katy proudly wore her new gold necklaces and a bright purple skirt that Annie had made for her own daughter when she was little.

Annie kept taking pictures of both of them. Bobby tried to look as evil as possible, but Katy couldn't suppress a big smile.

"I'm going to be a good pirate. Just like Pete," she said. "I sure hope I get to see him today."

Joey elbowed his mother. "She's carrying it a bit too far, don't you think?"

"Joey, don't worry about it. Besides, it didn't stop

you when you heard those voices. It will all work out."

Just then, Katy squealed, "They're coming! They're coming!"

Police cars with sirens wailing signaled the beginning of the parade. They were followed by fire engines and colorful floats. Boy Scouts and Girl Scouts marched by, while kids from karate schools and gymnastics classes kicked and twirled. Next there were belly dancers, soldiers, veterans, Shriners, and clowns.

Politicians rode by waving to the crowds from open convertibles, and local businessmen threw candy to the kids from their colorfully decorated cars and trucks. There were motorcycles, and bicycles, and wagons, and tractors, and horses. The high school band marched by, and some people even dressed up like giant shrimp. It seemed like everyone in town was there.

But the best was saved for last. They heard it before they saw it. A loud resounding boom echoed through the streets of Fernandina Beach.

"What's that?" Katy said.

"The pirates are coming!" George told her. "They

have a cannon on their ship, and they're coming right down the middle of the street!"

"Are they good pirates or bad pirates?" she asked.

"Oh, I think these are all pretty good ones. But just in case, your brothers and I will be right here. No one's threatening our women. Right, mates?"

"Right," both boys declared and flexed their arm muscles. "I'm right here, Katy," Joey added.

The first ship was black with a white skull and crossbones painted on the front. Two pirates were in the

front of the ship firing the cannon. A captured female pirate was being held hostage in a jail cell in the center of the ship. Smiling and waving to the crowd, she didn't seem to be too upset.

The second ship, called *Amelia's Revenge*, was much larger and had a redheaded mermaid carved on the bow. It also had a cannon. A few pirates rode on the ship and others were walking beside it. Several pirates ran into the crowd, snarling and waving their swords. Both scurvy-looking men and sassy women pirates threw candy and colorful bead necklaces to the kids. One pirate was swinging a rope that looked like a hangman's noose, and another had a patch over his eye. They were all having a good time.

Katy anxiously searched the faces of all the pirates. "I guess he's not here," she said a little sadly. Joey put his arm around her and patted her shoulder.

Ka-boom! Screaming girls, crying babies, and barking dogs were left behind as the pirate ships moved loudly out of sight.

Chapter 21
A Pirate Invasion

The rest of the weekend was a flurry of activities. They finally got to go to the beach on Friday. Joey got sunburned when he kept forgetting to apply sunscreen. Bobby called him Rudolf because of his red nose.

Bobby started to build a sand castle, but then decided to make it into a pirate ship. He asked Katy to find some sticks to use for the masts, and Jennifer fashioned a sail out of some newspaper.

Katy collected a bucketful of shells. Those with holes could be made into necklaces, she said.

"I might make a tiara too, and be the Princess of the Sea," she said.

"And I'll be the King of the Pirates," Bobby said. "All the other pirates will have to swear allegiance to me. I'll collect portions of their treasures and build a big palace on a tropical island. They can all live there when they aren't on the high seas doing their pirate thing."

"Would they be good pirates or bad pirates?" Katy asked.

"They'd be good pirates, of course, except when they're off stealing things," he said matter-of-factly.

He started digging a moat around the ship so it wouldn't get washed away by the incoming tide. Katy tied her beach towel around her neck like a train to a wedding dress. She wore her mother's sun visor on the top of her head, standing it straight up so it looked like a crown.

"Bobby, why do you like pirates so much?" she asked.

He thought about it for awhile.

"I dunno. I guess it's the adventure. They sail off to faraway places and meet all kinds of exciting people." Then he added, "And they get to wear really cool clothes."

Soon Jennifer said it was time to leave. "We need to get back and get cleaned up for the pirate invasion tonight."

Back at Annie's, they took showers to wash off the saltwater and sand. Bobby put on his pirate costume, but Katy said she didn't want to be a part of any invasion that might scare the little children.

Jennifer and the kids drove downtown, as Annie and George had already gone to help in one of the food booths. They had a hard time finding a parking space on the crowded streets. Centre Street was blocked off with barricades, and many of the artists were already setting up the booths for the Fine Arts and Crafts Show that would begin the next day.

They parked several blocks away and walked

toward the crowded waterfront. Music was booming from the riverfront stage, and the smells of fish cooking drifted toward them. Vendors were busy selling all kinds of food, including shrimp, fish, crawfish, French fries, hush-puppies, barbeque, hamburgers, corn dogs, hot dogs, and funnel cakes.

"I want a funnel cake," Bobby shouted.

"You can have one for dessert, after you've had some dinner," Jennifer said.

They ate at a picnic table by the water. Bobby bought a funnel cake and shared it with his sister. Then they walked around looking at all the booths, including one with all kinds of pirate items. Bobby bought a few more trinkets to add to his costume.

Katy wanted to see the Shrimp Festival princesses who were being introduced on the stage.

"Aren't they beautiful? Maybe I can be a princess some day," she said wistfully.

Later, they found Annie and George. Annie said she knew a good place to watch the pirate invasion and fireworks, so they followed her to a vacant spot along the waterfront.

By then, they were pretty tired. Katy was sleepy and Bobby complained of a stomach ache. George said he thought Bobby's fish might still be swimming around in his stomach, but Jennifer knew it was the funnel cake.

They watched the pirates, full of mischief, arrive on a decorated boat at the end of Centre Street. Teenage girls screamed as the pirates invaded the city, and young children ran to their mothers. It was a wild and crazy evening, and everyone had a good time—especially the pirates.

After the pirates' invasion, the fireworks began. Bright bursts of color exploded over the Amelia River. Oohs and aahs could be heard as the sky lit up over and over again. After the big finale, they walked back to the van with streams of people. George carried Katy who had fallen asleep.

"I think they got worn out at the beach today." Jennifer said. "We'll have to take it easy tomorrow."

Chapter 22
Katy's Pirate

The next day was Saturday. Jennifer told the kids to pack up all their belongings, as they would be heading back to Jacksonville that afternoon. She wanted to see some of the arts and crafts at the festival and talk to some of the artists, but planned to get home before dark.

Annie fixed them a big breakfast of scrambled eggs, bacon, and biscuits.

"It's sure been nice having you here," she said to Jennifer. "We've enjoyed having kids in the house again. I hope you'll come back again." She gave Jennifer copies of the pictures she had taken at the parade.

Katy said it was the best vacation she ever had and gave Annie a big hug. She thanked her for the purse and for showing her how to make jewelry.

Bobby suggested that she make lots of necklaces

and sell them to all her friends.

"You could make a fortune, and we could all take a cruise to the Caribbean and live on an island. I might find some buried treasure down there, too."

"Hold on," Joey said. "You found one coin. One! That is not a treasure."

"Yea, but it's a start," Bobby said. "Like everyone always says, you've got to start somewhere. So this is just the beginning for me. I'm going to …"

Jennifer interrupted him. "You're going to go take your things out to the van. Then we're going to return to reality, because you have to go to school on Monday. Now scoot."

They loaded the van, said their goodbyes to Annie and George. Bobby thanked George for telling him the stories about pirates and buried treasure. Joey said he enjoyed the ghost tour and the trip to the museum. They all waved as they drove away and headed downtown one last time. Again, they had to park several blocks away and walk to Centre Street.

The boys took Katy over to the Fun Zone, where

there were activities for kids, while Jennifer talked to several of the artists.

As they walked back to the van, Katy said she would have a booth some day and sell her jewelry. She said she'd also like to be a Miss Shrimp Festival princess and ride on a float and get a real tiara.

Bobby said he was going to join the Pirate Club and be part of the invasion.

"I'll have to practice my pirate talk," he said. "Arrr!"

Joey said he would like to go fishing the next time they visited Amelia Island. The captain of one of the charter boats had told him he could apply for a summer job on one of the boats when he got a little older.

Suddenly Katy squealed and started waving frantically.

A tall pirate with a broad grin on his face walked directly over to her. Joey started to grab Katy's hand but she pulled away from him and went running up to the pirate.

"Hi, Pete. I hoped I'd see you again," she said.

"Hello, Katy," he said, putting his hands on his hips and looking her up and down. "You look mighty pretty today."

"Thank you, sir," she said with a curtsey.

Joey stood there with his mouth open. He looked at his mother in disbelief and then back at the pirate. Jennifer was just as surprised. Bobby stepped forward and said, "Are you real, mister?"

"Yes, I believe I am. Wanna pinch me?"

"Ah, no. I believe you," he said as he backed away.

Pete bent down low and whispered to Katy.

"I've decided to fix up the old house and stick around awhile. I hope you'll come see me the next time you come to Amelia Island."

She nodded her head that she would. Then he lifted one of the gold necklaces he had around his neck.

"Here's a little token to remember me by," he said, as he placed the necklace around her neck. He turned to Joey and Bobby and said, "You boys take care of this little lady, you hear."

Both boys were speechless, but nodded that they would.

He patted Katy on the head, winked at her, then turned and walked away.

Katy stood there, fingering the necklace as she watched him go. Then she turned and faced her family with one hand on her hip.

"See, I told you he was a good pirate," she said, as

she looked from face to face. They all stared back at her, and then at each other, and then started to laugh.

"Yes, you did," her mother said. She grabbed Katy's hand, "Let's go home."

As they walked back to the van, Joey and Bobby hooked arms and started singing, *"Yo ho, Yo ho, a pirate's life for me…"*

"Mom, this is the best spring break ever," Katy said. "Can we come back again?"

"Of course," she said. "But remember, there are many other places to visit."

"Hmm. I wonder where our next adventure will be," Katy said. She smiled at her mother. "Let's go join the boys. We finally found a song that Bobby will sing."

They ran to catch up with the boys, hooked their arms together, and sang and laughed their way down the street.

THE END

About the Author

Jane R. Wood has been writing since elementary school when her 4th grade teacher encouraged her to write poetry. She later used her writing skills as a high school English teacher, a newspaper writer, and a television producer. Her first book, *Voices in St. Augustine*, was published in 2004.

Jane Wood was born in Astoria, Oregon, but moved to Florida when she was ten. She has always loved history, and chooses places that have a rich, colorful history for the settings of her books. Many of the people, places, and events mentioned in this book are based on historic fact or local legend. The characters of Joey and Bobby and their exploits are based on her two grown sons, Jonathan and Brian.

Mrs. Wood and her husband Terry live in Jacksonville, Florida, not far from Amelia Island. You can visit her website at www.janewoodbooks.com.